Poppy Love
Star Turn

NATASHA MAY

illustrated by
SHELAGH MCNICHOLAS

WALKER
BOOKS

With thanks to Neil Kelly and the students of
Rubies Dance Centre
N.M.

With thanks to Carolyn, Julia, Kirsty and Ann at
Bell's Dance Centre
S.N.

First published 2009 by Walker Books Ltd
87 Vauxhall Walk, London SE11 5HJ

2 4 6 8 10 9 7 5 3 1

Text © 2009 Veronica Bennett
Illustrations © 2009 Shelagh McNicholas

The author and illustrator have asserted their moral rights
in accordance with the Copyright, Designs and Patents Act 1988

This book has been typeset in ITC Giovanni

Printed and bound in Great Britain by Clays Ltd, St Ives plc

British Library Cataloguing in Publication Data:
a catalogue record for this book is available from the British Library

ISBN 978-1-4063-1665-0

www.walker.co.uk

Contents

Old Time Dancing

Poppy Love loved ballroom dancing.

She and her partner, Zack Bishop, went to Miss Johnson's dance lessons at the Blue Horizon Dance Studio, and had already passed some medal tests in both ballroom and Latin American dancing.

One day, when Poppy, Zack and the others were practising the dances for their next medal tests, Miss Johnson ended the

Competition Class a little early, and gathered the children around her. From her bag she took a folded piece of paper. "This," she said, her bright eyes darting from one child to another, "is an invitation!"

"Yay! A party!" yelled Sam, who never missed the chance to yell.

"Shush, Sam!" said Miss Johnson. "Mr Miller, the manager at Great Oaks, has invited you all to dance for the residents there, on Sunday afternoon."

There was a short silence, then the children all began to talk at once. "Which dances will we be doing?" asked Luke.

"What are we going to wear?" asked Rosie.

"What are residents?" asked Poppy.

"Will there be any food?" asked Sam.

"What's Great Oaks?" asked Emma, who hadn't lived in Brighton very long.

"Can I come?" asked Debbie, who was also new, "even though I don't know many dances yet?"

Miss Johnson put her hands over her ears. "I can't answer you all at once!" she said, laughing. "Great Oaks is a retirement home," she explained to Emma. "It's that red brick building, surrounded by tall trees, just down the road from here."

Poppy often looked
at Great Oaks when she was
on her way to or from the dance studio,
and wondered what it was like to live there.
Sometimes there would be a minibus parked
outside to take the people who lived there
on trips. Sometimes in the summer Poppy
would see someone with white hair at an
open window, and in the winter the lights
in the downstairs rooms looked
bright and cheerful.

"And yes, Debbie," added
Miss Johnson, "of course
you can come." Then she
read out the invitation.

The residents of
Great Oaks Retirement Home
cordially invite the children of
the Blue Horizon Dance Studio
to give a demonstration of ballroom dancing
at two o'clock on Sunday.
Refreshments will be provided.

The children looked at each other.
"Pardon?" said Zack, and they all laughed.

"The words are formal," explained Miss Johnson, "because that kind of language is traditional in a written invitation. Residents just means the people who live there, and cordially means being friendly, and refreshments means food, Sam."

"So when you reply to the invitation," said Poppy, "will you use those traditional words too?"

"Of course," said Miss Johnson. "Older people aren't the only ones with good manners."

"What will you say?" asked Zack curiously.

"Say we can't wait for Sunday!" suggested Sam.

Miss Johnson laughed. "Don't worry, I'll say something like that."

"This is going to be fun!" said Poppy and Cora and Emma together, making everyone laugh again.

Mr Miller, the manager of Great Oaks, was a tall man who wore his glasses on a chain around his neck. "Welcome, welcome!" he said, shaking Miss Johnson's hand and smiling at the children. "We're all ready for you."

He led them
into a large,
carpeted room.
On chairs and
sofas all around the sides
sat the audience. Poppy
could see that this was a very
special occasion at Great Oaks.
The ladies wore their best clothes and
their hair looked freshly curled. The men were
neatly turned out too, with collars and ties,
and smart jackets or suits. Everyone clapped
when Miss Johnson and the children entered
the room. Poppy was surprised at how many
people were there – it was quite a crowd!

She didn't feel nervous, though. She was
wearing her pretty blue dance dress with a
blue ribbon in her hair and neat white socks.

And she knew the dances well, because they were the three dances she and Zack were practising for their next medal test – the rumba, the salsa and the foxtrot.

"It'll be weird dancing on a carpet!" said Zack in Poppy's ear as he held up her hand and they walked out for the salsa.

Salsa meant "sauce" in Spanish. Poppy thought the name summed up the dance very well. Just as putting sauce on food livened it up, the salsa livened everything up. Dancers, audience, musicians – no one could keep still once the salsa music started.

Even though the thick carpet slowed them down a little, Poppy and the other children swayed and spun around the room, doing the bobbing, twisting salsa steps

until they were out of breath.
The audience smiled and
clapped, swaying in
time to the salsa music.
Some were even laughing,
and "dancing" with their
arms. And at the end, they
applauded and whooped so
loudly Poppy was amazed.

"This is the best audience we've ever had!"
she said to Cora.

"I'm loving this!" said Cora.
"What if we could do it again next
week? That would be so great!"

Miss Johnson bowed too. She
held out her hand to present
her dancers, and the audience
made even more noise.

"Now then, ladies and gentlemen," said
Miss Johnson when she could speak, "if you
enjoyed that, I'm sure you'll enjoy another
Latin American dance. The rumba!" And she
started the CD player.

Poppy loved the rumba music. People
often called the rumba the dance of love, but
to Poppy all dances were the dance of love,
because she loved them so much. What was
so lovely about the rumba music was the
soft, trembling sound the musicians made
with their guitars and trumpets. Poppy loved
the swishing of the brush the drummer used
instead of drumsticks, which made her want
to "swish" herself from side to side as if she
were part of the music itself.

She knew she looked nice in her blue
dress. Cora was in a pale yellow dress, and

Sophie in a pink one. They had matching ribbons in their hair, and Zack, Luke and Sam had ties the same colour as their partners' dresses. But the whole class was there, so the three boys danced with other girls of their age too. The older girls danced with each other and with Miss Johnson.

For competitions, Miss Johnson always wore black, because the judges were supposed to look at the child she was dancing with, and not at her. But this wasn't a competition, it was just for fun. To to the children's delight, Miss Johnson had put on her dark blue sparkly dance dress and her silver strappy shoes. Poppy thought she looked beautiful.

When the rumba ended there was more enthusiastic applause.

"This is much better than telly!" exclaimed one of the ladies. She had a white lacy blouse and a pink skirt, and a ribbon in her hair. "Just like the old days, before we even had telly!"

"No telly!" Sam stopped in the middle of his bow and looked at the lady in surprise. "But telly's been around for ever, hasn't it?"

The lady shook her head, and so did some of the other ladies sitting near her. They all began to talk at once, telling Sam that when they were young TV hadn't been invented. "It didn't come in until after the war," said one of the gentlemen, who had a brown suit and shiny shoes. "And by that time, I'd already been in the army and got married!"

"Wow!" exclaimed Sam. He and the other children were astonished. "What did you do, if you had no TV to watch?"

"Well, now that you ask," said the gentleman who had spoken, "we were always reading. And we went to football matches, and listened to the radio ... and we danced!" Leaning on the arm of the chair, he got to his feet. "Anyone care to join me?"

Miss Johnson smiled as she changed the CD. "Here's one you'll know," she said to the man in the brown suit. "One of the most popular dances ever. The foxtrot. Shall we?"

She held up her arms, and she and the man began to dance the foxtrot.

The foxtrot was a ballroom dance that had to be danced very smoothly. Unlike the Latin American dances, with their bouncing, swinging steps, or the other ballroom dances with their dipping, swaying and striding, Miss Johnson always said that the foxtrot had to look as if you were skating on ice.

"Smooth, smooth, smooth," Poppy repeated to herself as Zack took her in the ballroom hold, with one hand on her back and the other holding her hand. They'd done it so often before, she knew they could do it well now.

But they'd never done a foxtrot on carpet before. Soon after they started, Poppy could see by Zack's face that he was thinking the same thing. How do you "skate" on a thick carpet?

Everyone was having the same trouble. The dance looked OK, Poppy was sure, but it didn't really look like a foxtrot should look. She was disappointed. What a pity they couldn't do their beautiful, gliding foxtrot!

Suddenly, an elderly gentleman in a tweed jacket, with thick glasses slipping down his nose, stood up and bowed to her. "May I cut in?" he asked.

Poppy knew that cutting in meant starting to dance with a girl who was already dancing with someone else. Zack gave Poppy a "might as well!" look and let go of her, and the man with the glasses took his place. The man was too tall for Poppy to reach his shoulder with her hand, so she held his elbow.

Despite his age, his steps were light and he steered Poppy easily between the other couples. His jacket was tickly and he smelled of mints. But Poppy liked being taken around the floor by someone who thought of dancing as an ordinary part of life, not something you watch on TV. And to think there wasn't even any TV to watch when he was a young man!

Most surprising of all, the man in the tweed jacket made a better job of dancing smoothly on the carpet than any of the children. "What you need to do, you see," he told Poppy, "is do each step just ahead of the music, because the carpet slows you down. By the time you do the next step, the music's caught up with you again, and then you go ahead of it, and so on."

Poppy tried doing this. It felt odd to be keeping ahead of the music on purpose, but to her surprise, it worked.

"Perfect," said the man, smiling. "You're a fine dancer, my dear."

Poppy felt very proud, but was too shy to say anything.

"You know," the man went on, "sixty years ago, we would put on the record player, or someone would play the piano, or there would be music on the radio, and we'd dance. The foxtrot, the waltz, the quickstep…"

"At a party, you mean?" asked Poppy, trying to imagine what a party sixty years ago would be like.

"Sometimes," he replied, "but whenever we wanted, really. We didn't need a proper dance floor – we got used to dancing on carpets."

"That must have been great," said Poppy.

The old man laughed. "It was. And you know, not many people had phones, or cars, and there certainly weren't any computers. But we enjoyed ourselves just as much as youngsters do today. And it's wonderful to see you young ones dancing the old dances."

"I love dancing!" Poppy told him.

It didn't take long for other residents of Great Oaks, men and women, to stand up and join in the foxtrot. Zack danced with a lady in a green dress whose steps were correct even though she was wearing fluffy slippers.

And although Poppy had
done the foxtrot hundreds
of times before, dancing it
with the man in the tweed
jacket had transported her
back in time to when films
were in black and

white, and
ballroom dancing music
came out of the radio. They
had danced it the way it
was meant to be danced.

When the music ended,
Poppy's partner
stood back

and bowed politely. "Thank you,
miss," he said, holding out his
hand. "That's made my day."

Poppy took hold of her partner's hand and shook it solemnly. "Doing the foxtrot with you was really brilliant!" she said.

"I'm so glad you enjoyed it," said the man, straightening up. "Will you come and dance with us again?"

"Yes please!" said Poppy.

Bossa Nova Bridesmaid

Poppy's Auntie Jill, who lived with the Love family in their flat at the top of the Hotel Gemini, was engaged to Simon Forrester. The wedding was getting nearer and nearer, and Poppy was getting more and more excited about being a bridesmaid.

"Only two weeks to go!" she told Zack one Friday when they arrived at the studios for their private lesson with Miss Johnson.

"You should see my dress! It's pink, and I've got pink shoes, and a garland for my hair, and— "

"I know, you already told me," interrupted Zack, rolling his eyes impatiently. He was only joking, though. He was almost as excited about the wedding as Poppy was. "It's the food I'm looking forward to, not the dresses."

"I know," said Poppy, rolling her eyes. "You already told me."

Miss Johnson held up a CD in a colourful case. "Do you know what bossa nova is?" she asked.

When Zack and Poppy shook their heads, she explained. "It's a type of music that comes from Brazil," she said, sliding the CD into the machine. "Listen."

The room filled with the sound of
trumpets, guitars and drums playing a soft,
rumbling music with a Latin American
beat, rather like the music for the
cha-cha-cha or the rumba. But
then a woman's voice began to
sing in a language with lots of
murmuring "sh" sounds in it.

"That language is Portuguese,"
said Miss Johnson.

The song seemed to wash over Poppy like
a wave on the beach, and before she knew
it she was moving in time with the
rhythm, swaying her hips. "I love
this!" she exclaimed.

"Good." Miss Johnson
turned down the volume
and looked at them keenly.

"I thought you two might like to learn the club dance – the bossa nova – that goes with the music. It's called a club dance because in the nightclubs of Brazil years ago, bossa nova was a new kind of beat and a new kind of dance," she explained. "'Nova' means 'new', in fact. It was very popular in the USA, too. That's why some bossa nova songs are in English, like this next one."

The next song began. Poppy listened to the romantic words and the calm, dreamy music. "What's this song called?" she asked.

"'The Look of Love'," replied Miss Johnson. "It was one of the biggest bossa nova hits ever. I always think the words and music are just perfect for each other."

"Like my Auntie Jill and Simon!" said Poppy, who hadn't quite forgotten about the wedding.

Then she thought of something, and caught hold of Zack's arm. "Why don't we ask if the band can play this song at the wedding?" she suggested.

Before he could speak, she thought of something else. "And we could dance the bossa nova for the wedding guests!"

And then she thought of yet another thing, and began to skip up and down. "Auntie Jill knows all the dances already, but we could secretly teach the bossa nova to Simon, so he can do it with her to this song! It would be such a nice surprise for her! A perfect song for a wedding, and a perfect dance!"

"*We* don't even know the dance yet," pointed out Zack.

"You soon will," said Miss Johnson. "That's a great idea, Poppy." She started "The Look of Love" again. "Let's do our warm-up to the bossa nova music, then you two can come and stand in front of the mirror and follow what I do."

The dance was unlike anything Poppy and Zack had done before. Miss Johnson showed them how to put one of their hands on their stomach and hold the other one out to the side, then sway their hips while they took steps forwards and backwards.

"Partners can touch hands if they want to, or the lady can put her

hand on the man's chest, or his shoulder,"
Miss Johnson told them. "But they don't
have to. You can also do it alone, which
is why it was such a popular club dance.
Everyone could dance, whether they had a
partner or not. And you stay in one place
while you're dancing, so you can talk. There's
not much room to move on a crowded dance
floor in a nightclub!"

Poppy and Zack faced each other and
began to do the bossa nova. The steps were
simple. The hardest part was remembering
to sway their hips at the same
time as they moved their feet
backwards and forwards on
the same spot. They did it
for a few minutes, getting
better and better at it.

But then Miss Johnson looked at the clock. "We'd better leave the bossa nova now," she said, "and practise your dances for the gold star test. Only a few weeks to go!"

The gold star test was important. Poppy and Zack were doing three dances – the rumba, the foxtrot and the salsa. If Poppy passed them all, the medals for them would be added to the nine she already had, and she would be awarded her twelve-dance gold star. That meant she would be able to enter the competition to qualify to dance against all the other gold star holders at the Nationwide Finals.

It was an important test for Zack too. He had to pass four dances, as he'd failed the paso doble last time. He was going to take this dance again with Emma, because he seemed to dance it better with her than with Poppy. If he passed it, and passed the three new dances, he'd get his gold star too.

"But the bossa nova is such fun!" protested Zack.

Miss Johnson looked at the timer on the CD player. "All right, then," she said. "Go on doing it until the end of this track. Then we really must stop."

Just like Miss Johnson had said, because they were facing each other and dancing in the same spot, Poppy and Zack could easily talk as they did the bossa nova.

"How are we going to teach Simon this dance without your auntie finding out?" asked Zack.

"Don't worry," Poppy told him. "Auntie Jill often goes off on Saturdays to dancing competitions." Her aunt had been a champion ballroom dancer, and still worked as a competition judge. "We can go round to Simon's house tomorrow if he's not working in his restaurant."

"Come on, then," said Miss Johnson as the bossa nova music ended. "Are you ready? Let's go for that gold star!"

Mum thought Poppy's idea was great. "I can just see Simon doing a bossa nova!" she said with a laugh when Poppy told her about it the next day.

"But we need to teach it to him without Auntie Jill knowing," said Poppy. "And he's always so busy."

Mum looked thoughtful, and checked her watch. "At this time on a Saturday he'll be in his office at the restaurant." She found the number and began to tap it into the phone.

"What are you going to say to him?" asked Poppy.

"I'm going to ask if I can take you and Zack to his house for some bossa nova lessons later today," replied Mum. Then she put up her hand to shush Poppy. "Simon, it's Julie," she said into the phone. "Have you got a minute? I want to ask you something."

While Mum spoke to Simon, Poppy wandered along the hallway to her bedroom. Next to it, the door to Auntie Jill's bedroom was slightly open. Through it Poppy could see the page boy suit Simon's little nephew Ben was going

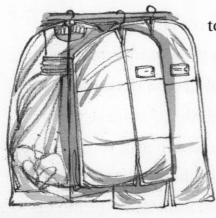 to wear, and her own bridesmaid's dress. They were hanging in plastic bags on the outside of her aunt's wardrobe.

Auntie Jill's wedding dress, Poppy knew, was hidden away inside the wardrobe so that Simon wouldn't see it before the big day, which was supposed to be unlucky.

Poppy went into her room and looked at herself in the practice mirror that almost covered one wall. She was still wearing the clothes she'd been to class in that morning – a short, swirly skirt and a white T-shirt with "Blue Horizon Dance Studio" on the front. Her dark hair had started to come loose from her ponytail, because of all the energy she'd put into the rumba, the foxtrot and the salsa this morning. And the bossa nova, of course.

She began to do the bossa nova steps, imagining that instead of her practice clothes she was wearing the beautiful pink bridesmaid's dress, and that her hair was swept up under a garland of flowers. It might look unusual, but it would be fun!

Mum put her head round the bedroom door. "Simon's free at five o'clock, and Jill won't be home till seven. You'll be back here by then, so she won't suspect a thing. I'll just phone Zack's mum. Isn't this exciting!"

* * *

Poppy couldn't believe the day of the wedding had come at last – here they were outside the church! Her older brother, Tom, was wearing a suit for the very first time. It was dark grey, and he had a white rose in his buttonhole, a white shirt with silver cufflinks and a silver-grey tie. His curly hair, which usually stuck out behind his ears, was held down with styling gel.

"You look like a different person," Poppy told him as he opened the door of the limousine and she stepped out.

"So do you," said Tom, smiling. "I don't know who, but definitely not my little sister!"

Poppy didn't feel like herself either. In her pink dress and shoes, with roses and lilies in her hair and a bouquet of the same flowers in her hand, she felt like a princess on her way to a ball. Mum had told her the dress was made of a fabric called taffeta, which caught the light as Poppy moved, so that it glimmered with many different shades of pink.

The first time she'd tried the dress on and Mum had fixed the garland in her hair, Poppy had stared and stared at the girl in the mirror, who didn't look like Poppy Love at all.

"Poppy's right," said Granny, who
had followed Poppy out of the car.
"You look very smart, Tom."

"Well, I'm an usher," said Tom seriously.
"I have to show the wedding guests where to
sit in the church."

"Little Tom's an usher too," Poppy told her
grandmother as they helped Simon's smallest
nephew, Ben, from the car. "I wonder how
he's getting on."

Poppy was good friends with Ben's brother,
Little Tom, who was her age and had recently
begun to go with her to dance lessons at
the Blue Horizon Dance Studio. Because of
Poppy's brother being called Tom too, Little
Tom had soon got used to the nickname.
He was a shy boy, and Poppy knew he'd be
nervous.

"I'm fine, thanks."

Poppy turned round, and there was Little Tom, smiling broadly. "Oh!" she exclaimed. "You look so smart!"

Little Tom was wearing a suit just like Poppy's brother's. "How does that stay on?" he asked Poppy, looking with interest at the garland around her hair.

"With lots of hairpins," Poppy told him.

"I'm glad I'm not a girl," said Little Tom as he went to greet another party of guests. He looked down at his young brother. "See you later, Ben. You do what Poppy tells you, won't you?"

Ben was a page boy, so Granny had brought him with Poppy in the bridesmaids' limousine. Grandad and Auntie Jill herself would arrive in the bride's limousine, and

then Ben and Poppy
would follow the bride
up the aisle. He looked
sweet, dressed in velvet
trousers and a waistcoat.

She took his hand. "Ready?"
she asked. "The bride's car's going to be here
any minute."

"Look!" said Ben, pointing. "Here it is!"

Poppy held her breath as the limousine
drew up, the door opened and the bride
stepped out.

Auntie Jill looked beautiful – more
beautiful than she had ever looked before.
Poppy had seen her looking lovely in sparkly
dance dresses and long evening gowns, or
even simple summer dresses. But the dress
she wore today – a special dress, her wedding

dress – made her look more beautiful than Poppy could have ever dreamed.

The dress was made of the purest silk, in the purest white. It reached the floor in the front, just showing the tips of Auntie Jill's white shoes. At the back the skirt lengthened into a train, which Poppy's aunt held up by a loop around her wrist. The low neckline, falling elegantly from Auntie Jill's delicate shoulders, looked perfect beneath the veil that covered her face. Under the veil, Poppy could just see her aunt's face, smiling for the photographer.

"I wonder if she's nervous," said Poppy to Granny.

"Grandad will be!" said Granny.

"When he gave your mum away at her wedding, he was so scared he couldn't sleep the night before."

Auntie Jill's bouquet, like Poppy's, was of lilies and roses. Grandad, looking very smart in his best suit with a rose in his buttonhole, and not nervous at all, walked beside his daughter to the church door. Auntie Jill let her train fall from her wrist, and Poppy and Ben picked it up, taking their places proudly behind the bride.

Poppy knew she would never forget the moment when the procession entered the church, and the guests turned round and gasped when they saw Auntie Jill. She knew she would never forget the sound of the music playing, and the feel of her bouquet in one hand, and the silken train in the other. Most of all, she knew she'd never forget Simon's face when he, too, turned round from where he waited before the altar, and first saw his beautiful bride.

"They look gorgeous!" thought Poppy as Auntie Jill lifted her veil, and she and Simon smiled at each other. "But more than that, they're so happy!"

The wedding reception was held in the Grand Hotel on the seafront in Brighton. Poppy thought it was a good name, because the reception was a very grand affair indeed.

The huge room was decorated with flowers and hung with ribbon bows. Delicious food was served by smartly dressed waiters and waitresses, and there were little cards and gifts on all the tables. In the centre of the main table, where Poppy sat beside the bride and groom, was the tallest iced cake Poppy had ever seen.

After the meal there were speeches, and the guests raised their champagne glasses to toast the newlyweds.

"I give you Mr and Mrs Simon Forrester!" announced the Master of Ceremonies, and everyone took a sip of champagne. Poppy had some, but she didn't

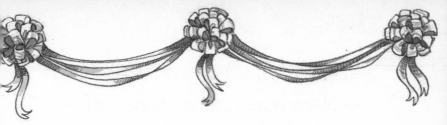

like it much. It tasted sour and tickled her nose. Then Simon made a speech, and at the end of it he raised his own glass to the bridesmaid and the page boy.

"To Poppy and Ben!" he said, and everyone stood up. Poppy was a little embarrassed as she took Ben's small, sticky hand and stood up too. But she also felt pleased.

"This is so great!" she said to Auntie Jill as they all sat down again.

At that moment the band struck up a waltz tune. Uncle Simon, looking very handsome in his grey wedding suit, stood up and offered Auntie Jill his hand. "May I have the pleasure of the first dance?" he asked.

Granny had told Poppy that it was the custom at weddings for the bride and groom to open the dancing with a waltz. They would dance alone at first, then be joined by other couples. Uncle Simon and Auntie Jill threaded their way between the tables to the dance floor, while the guests applauded. Poppy caught Zack's eye. He made a thumbs-up sign, and so did she. They were about to put into action what they'd been planning for the last two weeks.

Poppy's aunt and her new husband looked very good dancing together. Uncle Simon had learnt lots of dances from Auntie Jill and did them well. Now, of course, he'd secretly learnt a new dance from Poppy and Zack, too!

Zack and Poppy joined in the waltzing. The wedding guests smiled and whispered to each other, and some were filming with camcorders. Poppy tried to dance especially beautifully, knowing those films would be watched over and over again for a long time.

"Are you ready?" Poppy whispered to Zack, who nodded.

As the waltz music ended, the band's singer, a tall man in a white jacket, approached the microphone. "Ladies and gentlemen," he announced, "'The Look of Love'."

The band began to play the soft, rustling bossa nova music. Guests who had been waltzing began to move to the beat, uncertain what to do but not wishing to sit down. Most of them were looking at the bride and groom. As the singer began to sing the romantic words, Uncle Simon put one of his hands on his stomach and stretched out the other one in the bossa nova position. To Auntie Jill's astonishment, he began to sway his hips and move his feet backwards and forwards in the bossa nova step.

"This is my favourite bossa nova song!" exclaimed Auntie Jill, putting her own hand on her stomach and beginning to move her own hips. "Simon, how did you know? And how do you know the steps?"

Uncle Simon, who had a big smile on his face, shook his head. "Don't ask," he said. "Let's just dance!"

As they had planned, Zack stood behind Uncle Simon, doing the bossa nova steps and beckoning for the guests to copy what he was doing, and Poppy did the same behind Auntie Jill. Couple by couple, one by one, even three by three, everyone began to move to the bossa nova rhythm. Poppy's family, including her grandparents, joined in. Grandad, who had always liked dancing, was really good at it. "Granny and I did the bossa nova in the nineteen-sixties," he told Poppy. "Just watch us!"

Poppy couldn't help laughing as her grandparents danced the bossa nova. It wasn't that they looked funny – in fact they looked brilliant, Grandad in his wedding suit and Granny in her pretty navy blue and white jacket, and both of them wearing huge smiles. It was just that she was so pleased to see three

generations of her family dancing together. "Now I know why I've loved dancing ever since I was born," she said to Zack. "Just look at Grandad go!"

Little Tom soon picked up the dance and taught it to Ben, who looked so comical bossa nova-ing in his velvet trousers and white stockings that Poppy found herself laughing at that, too.

Auntie Jill was holding up her train with one hand, her other hand resting lightly on Uncle Simon's chest. As they swayed to the bossa nova rhythm they looked at each other as if there was no one else in the room. Poppy watched them, feeling very glad that her idea had worked, and "The Look of Love" had turned out to be the perfect song for a perfect wedding.

When the music ended, Uncle Simon suddenly swept Poppy off her feet and put her on his shoulders. The wedding guests applauded. She looked down at everyone gathered on the dance floor and waved, knowing she would remember this moment for ever, without needing to look at a recording.

"Poppy!"

It was Auntie Jill, holding up her arms to help Uncle Simon lower Poppy to the ground. When he'd done so, Auntie Jill crouched down, her white silk skirt crumpling all around her on the floor, and looked into Poppy's face. "This was all your idea, wasn't it?" she asked, smiling. "Simon says you and Zack made him practise the bossa nova until his feet hurt."

Poppy smiled too. She felt like she'd hardly stopped smiling all day. "He was terrible at it when we started," she told her aunt, "but he learnt it quite quickly once he'd stopped messing about."

"Well," said Auntie Jill. "'The Look of Love' was a terrific idea." She kissed Poppy's cheek. "Thank you, Poppy. You know what Simon just called you?"

Poppy looked up at Uncle Simon, who was grinning. "No, what?" she asked.

Auntie Jill and Uncle Simon exchanged a glance. Then, both together, they said, "You're our bossa nova bridesmaid!"

Stardance

The Blue Horizon Dance Studio was buzzing
with excitement.

Almost everyone in Miss Johnson's
competition class was doing a medal test
today, and the studio was full of children
with sweatshirts and cardigans over their
dance clothes, warming up and practising
their steps one last time. As she danced,
Poppy thought about her twelve-medal

display board, which she'd
brought with her. It was in
her dance bag along with
Lucky, her lucky toy puppy.

If she and Zack danced
their best today, the three remaining
spaces round the outside of the board would
soon be filled by her foxtrot, rumba and salsa
medals, and the one in the middle would
hold her gold star. The thought was making
her feel rather nervous.

"Come on," said Zack, "we're warm
enough now. Let's run through the routines."

Poppy took off her cardigan. She was
wearing her green dance dress, and Mum
had put her hair in a bun with a green
ribbon. Today was a test, not
a competition, but it was still

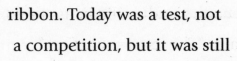

important to look like a ballroom dancer.
So Mum had touched Poppy's eyelashes
with mascara and her lips with
strawberry-flavoured lip gloss.

Under his sweatshirt Zack had on
his usual black trousers and white shirt, and
a plain black bow tie. Poppy could see that
his clothes were freshly washed and ironed,
and that he'd taken ages doing his hair.

It was a big day for Zack. He was going
to re-take the paso doble test, dancing with
Emma. Because Poppy hadn't been practising
it with him, she didn't know if he'd
improved. She hoped so much that he had!

They went through their three dances,
then Zack let go of Poppy's hand and looked
around the studio. "I'd better find Emma,"
he said. "The re-takes are first."

"OK," said Poppy. "I'd better find Luke, then."

Luke had failed the quickstep last time. Although he was usually Cora's partner, he'd found he was more comfortable in the dance with Poppy, so she was going to do the quickstep with him today for the medal test.

"Hey, Luke!" she called when she saw him.

"Hey, Poppy," replied Luke. "We're on first. Ready?"

"Can't wait!" This was quite true. Poppy was glad to be getting her dance with Luke over first. She was nervous enough about her own dances, and didn't want to let him down.

As they ran through the quickstep, Poppy caught sight of Emma and Zack practising the paso doble. Emma looked very pretty in a pink dress trimmed with white. Poppy felt pleased that Zack's partner had dressed nicely to dance with him, even though she herself wasn't taking any medal tests today.

"You look great!" Poppy told her as they passed each other.

"So do you," said Emma. "Like minty ice cream. Someone give me a spoon!"

Poppy knew Emma was saying jokey things to try to calm her nerves, but it didn't help much. She just couldn't smile.

When Miss Johnson called for the end of practice, Zack came over and looked closely at Poppy. "All right, Pop?" he asked.

"A bit nervous," said Poppy. "What about you?"

"I think I'll feel better when the paso's over," he told her.

"Good luck," said Poppy.

"Good luck to you and Luke, too," said Zack, and they high-fived as they always did before they danced.

Miss Johnson introduced the examiner, Mrs Travers. Poppy remembered her friendly smile and silver hair from their last medal test. "Everyone ready?" she asked. "Let's do the quickstep first."

For the first few bars of the music Luke's shoulders were stiff and Poppy knew he was nervous. But she tried to make her steps as "quick" as she could – light and bouncy without jumping too much. And soon Luke's shoulders softened and his freckly face began to smile. Poppy was relieved. She was sure he'd pass the quickstep this time.

When Mrs Travers announced the paso

doble, Poppy watched Zack walk to the middle of the floor with Emma, and take up his position. He was the bullfighter, and Emma was his cape. "Dance well, Zack!" she said under her breath.

He did dance well. All the practice he and Emma had done seemed to be paying off. Miss Johnson, who was standing in the corner by the CD player, watched them with shining eyes as they moved together in perfect time to the music, strutting and turning around the imaginary bull.

Zack looked happy when he and Emma came off the floor after the paso. He let go of Emma's hand and took Poppy's. "Ready?"

"Yep," she told him. "Let's do it."

The rest of the medal test flew past very quickly. In the two Latin American dances, the salsa and the rumba, Zack danced better than he'd ever danced before. When Poppy put out her hand, his hand was there to catch it. When she turned her head, his head turned at exactly the same moment. Side by side in the salsa, their steps were so together she almost felt like they were no longer two separate people. Zack was so sure that he'd got the paso doble right, it seemed he couldn't put a foot wrong in any of the dances.

And Poppy knew Mrs Travers was noting all this down.

As they waited for the foxtrot music to start, Poppy could feel that Zack's hands were trembling a little. Even though the Latin

American dances had gone so well, he was still nervous about the ballroom dance. The foxtrot was a smooth, lilting dance, with no jerky movements. As they waited for the right beat of the music to start on, Poppy hoped all their hours of practice would be worth it.

As soon as they took their first steps, Poppy knew that Zack was still dancing better than ever. He led the way around and between the other couples so well Poppy that was sure Mrs Travers would be impressed.

When the dance finished, Poppy felt strange. She was glad the test was over, but she also felt lively, as if she could do the whole thing again and not get tired. "You were totally amazing," she said to Zack as they changed their shoes. "You're bound to get your medals."

"*We're* bound to get them, you mean," said Zack. "We were exactly together in the salsa – did you notice?"

"Of course," said Poppy, opening her bag to get out her street shoes.

"Oh!" Zack had caught sight of the wooden frame of Poppy's medal display board, peeping out from behind Lucky. "You brought it with you!"

Shyly, Poppy took the board out of the bag. "I don't know why, really. It just felt like the right thing to do, I suppose."

Zack took it from her and gazed at it seriously. Poppy knew he had one at home that was almost the same. The only

difference was that she had the paso doble medal and he didn't.

"These boards are going to look great when they've got the gold star in the middle," he said. "I can't wait to enter the Stardance competition!"

The Stardance competition was for children who had passed all twelve medals and got their gold star. Poppy and Zack, along with other gold star holders from the South East of England, would be dancing at an event held in London in a few weeks' time.

Poppy smiled. It was lovely to see Zack so confident after he'd been so nervous. "Me too," she said, holding up her hand.

"Let's try and win it!" said Zack, slapping Poppy's hand.

"Do we ever do anything else?" asked Poppy, laughing.

* * *

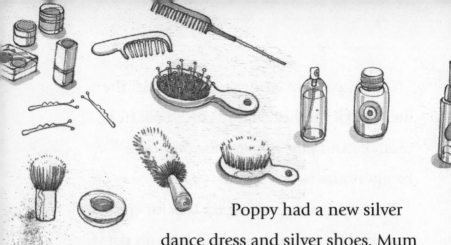

Poppy had a new silver dance dress and silver shoes. Mum and Auntie Jill had taken ages to spray her with fake tan, make up her face, and fix silver feathers in her slicked-down hair. With her white socks, tanned skin, dark hair and blue eyes, she looked so striking that passers-by turned to look at her as she and her family walked through the leisure centre where the competition was being held.

She wished her brother Tom could see her. But he was in secondary school now, and went to football practice on Sunday mornings.

"Sorry, Poppy," he'd said as they left the house. "I'll be cheering you on in my head, though. And Dad'll take lots of photos, like he always does."

Zack, who was wearing a black bow tie threaded with silver to match Poppy's dress, was so proud he looked ready to burst. "I love doing competitions!" he said happily as they went into the main hall to warm up. "I can't wait to do the Stardance Final in Blackpool!"

If gold star holders did well enough in local competitions, they could enter the Stardance Final held at the Nationwide Finals in Blackpool, against the other top Stardancers from all over the country.

Poppy found the thought of this exciting, but scary.

"We might not get through, you know," she told Zack.

"I bet we will," he said. "Look how well we did in that last medal test!"

It was true. Poppy and Zack's medal display boards each had all twelve medals round the outside now, and a gold star in the middle. And Mrs Travers had told Miss Johnson how well she thought Poppy and Zack had danced. She had also singled out Emma for praise, and mentioned to Miss Johnson that there was a lot of talent in her school.

They had a lot to live up to, because today, Mrs Travers was one of the judges.

"There she is!" whispered Poppy as she and

Zack passed in front of the judges' chairs.

Mrs Travers saw them, but made no sign that she knew them. Auntie Jill, who also judged competitions, had told Poppy that judges weren't being mean when they ignored people they knew. It was just that, to be fair, they had to treat everyone the same. That's why Poppy wasn't allowed to dance in any competition that Auntie Jill judged.

Poppy and Zack got through the first two rounds of the Stardance competition. Then they got through the semi-final. When the final was announced, they waited breathlessly for their numbers to be called … or not. Poppy could see Auntie Jill, and beside her Zack's mum, with her hand over her mouth. Next to her was Dad, hugging Mum tightly. They were all as breathless as

Poppy and Zack themselves.

"Number four-one-two," called the announcer, and a great cheer went up for Zack.

A long time seemed to go by. Poppy had almost given up hope, but then the announcer read out, "Number four-five-five," and a cheer went up for her, too.

As she and Zack bounded onto the dance floor with the other selected dancers, she caught a glimpse of Mum and Dad and the others, all in a row, standing up and clapping as hard as they could. Dad was whistling through his fingers, and everyone was stamping their feet. What a pity Tom had missed this!

"Look at our fan club!" said Zack as he and Poppy took up the opening position of the rumba. "This is getting embarrassing!"

Dancing in the Stardance competition needed something more than knowing the dances well. They had to perform the dances, showing the judges that they understood the look and style of each one.

The soft, romantic music of the rumba started, and Poppy began to sway her hips and move her feet to its rhythm. She placed her arms and fingers carefully, stretching her back and legs just like Miss Johnson had told her, as perfectly as she could.

Then she and Zack tripped lightly around the floor in the quickstep. Poppy thought she had never seen Zack's steps so springy, or his brown eyes so bright. He didn't seem nervous at all.

And when the samba started, Poppy knew that they were really performing. She could feel it in every roll, bend and turn of the dance, and in every swirl of her silver skirt.

At the end the applause was very loud. Miss Johnson hugged Poppy and Zack. "Well done!" she said happily. "You know, even if you don't get placed, just getting this far means you've qualified for the Nationwide Finals."

"I hope we don't come last, though," said Zack.

They didn't come last.

And they didn't come next to last, either. In fact, they didn't come in any of the next few places.

Zack gripped Poppy's hand tightly as the numbers for third place were read out. They weren't theirs. Just when Poppy thought she'd have to scream, or jump up and down, the announcer said, "Second place, numbers four-one-two and four-five-five," and she screamed and jumped up and down anyway.

It was the best they'd ever done in a competition. Poppy thought she might burst, she was so proud when they collected their silver shields. The man presenting them wasn't one of the judges – he belonged to the dance organization that was holding the competition.

"Thank you, thank you!" said Poppy in excitement as he gave her the little shield. Beside him stood Mrs Travers, who nodded and smiled at all the children as they took their prizes. Poppy smiled back at her.

They posed
for photographs
with the top three
couples. Dad snapped away,
taking as many pictures as he
could. Then their families gathered round,
eager to congratulate Poppy and Zack.

"I knew that dress would be lucky," said
Mum, whose eyes were glittering with tears.
"A silver shield for a silver dress!"

"And a silver bow tie," added Dad. "I
thought you danced brilliantly today, Zack."

"Thanks, Mr Love," said Zack, shyly but
proudly.

"Will you and Uncle Simon come
to Blackpool when we compete in the
Nationwide Finals?" Poppy asked Auntie Jill.
"And Little Tom? And Ben?"

"Just try and stop us!" said Auntie Jill. "I wouldn't miss it for the world!"

All of a sudden, Poppy found that she couldn't speak. Overcome with happiness and relief, she felt she was about to cry. So she just nodded, and squeezed Mum's hand. She realized that she felt very, very tired.

Dad lifted her up and carried her through the crowd to the car, and Mum gently strapped her into the back seat and kissed her forehead. Poppy tried to stay awake, so that this fantastic day would last as long as possible. But her eyes kept closing.

"Go to sleep, love," said Mum, putting a cushion behind Poppy's head. "It's a long journey home. And you've got an extra dance class tomorrow, to prepare for the Christmas show."

Poppy remembered how much fun Miss Johnson's Christmas show had been last year. She opened her eyes. "Will Tom come and see me in the Christmas show?" she asked Mum. "If I go to his football matches?"

Mum laughed. "Of course he will, even if you don't. Now, just sleep."

Poppy imagined the expression on her brother's face when she told him what had happened today, and smiled to herself. She settled her head more comfortably on the cushion. And in two minutes she was asleep, dreaming of silver dresses, silver shields, football boots – and Christmas.

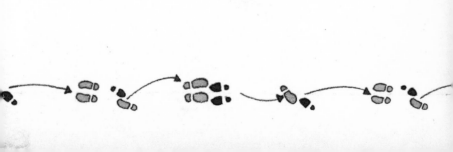

Natasha May loves dance of all kinds. When she was a little girl she dreamed of being a dancer, but also wanted to be a writer. "So writing about dancing is the best job in the world," she says. "And my daughter, who is a dancer, keeps me on my toes about the world of dance."

Shelagh McNicholas loves to draw people spinning around and dancing. Her passion began when her daughter, Molly, started baby ballet classes, "and as she perfected her dancing skills we would practise the jive, samba and quickstep all around the house!"